W9-AMR-702

DISNEY's
THE
LION KING

This is the story of a lion cub named Simba who grew up to become the Lion King. Read along with me as we embark on an exciting adventure. You will know it is time to turn the page when you hear this sound....Just follow along, and enjoy this wonderful tale about Simba and friends!

publications international, ltd.

A joyous day dawned in the Pride Lands. A lion prince had been born! The animals gathered at Pride Rock to celebrate the Circle of Life. They bowed low as the wise baboon Rafiki held Simba high. King Mufasa and Sarabi watched their cub proudly.

But one animal was missing from the crowd. Scar, Mufasa's brother, did not want to see his new nephew. "It must have slipped my mind," Scar told Mufasa.

Scar had hoped to become king when Mufasa's rule ended. Now he knew that Simba would become the next Lion King.

To try to get him out of the way, Scar set a trap for young Simba and his friend Nala. He tricked them into exploring an elephant graveyard. To make sure that Simba didn't come back, Scar sent three hungry hyenas to meet him.

Mufasa rescued the young cubs. He did not know about Scar'
trick. He only knew that he was disappointed in his son for takin
foolish chances.

"Look at the stars, Simba," said Mufasa. "The great kings of th
past look down on us from those stars. Just remember that those
kings will always be there to guide you—and so will I."

Scar was upset for a different reason: Simba was still alive. Scar led Simba to a deep canyon and started a stampede to crush him. Then he ran for Mufasa.

"Stampede! In the gorge! Simba's down there!" panted Scar. Mufasa tried to save Simba, but Scar pushed the Lion King into the stampede. Simba survived. Mufasa did not.

Simba did not see Scar's terrible deed, and Scar let him think that he was to blame for Mufasa's death.

"Simba, what have you done?" said Scar.

"It was an accident," cried Simba. "I didn't mean for it to happen. What am I going to do?"

"Run away and never return," Scar told him.

Simba ran until he collapsed. A friendly warthog named Pumbaa and a wily meerkat named Timon found him. They invited Simba to join their life of no worries. Simba grew up with these two friends as his family. Still, some nights as he looked at the stars, he remembered his father and felt lonely.

Then one day, Simba's past came crashin[g]
into his carefree life. Nala had been huntin[g]
for food—but she found Simba!

Nala was thrilled to see him. She quickly told Simba that he had to return to the Pride Lands. "Scar let the hyenas take over the Pride Lands. Everything's destroyed. You're our only hope."

Simba turned away. How could he ever return to the Pride Lands? He looked into the starry night. This time, he heard his father's voice.

"Look inside yourself, Simba," said Mufasa. "You are more than what you have become. You must take your place in the Circle of Life. You are my son and the one true king."

Simba returned to the Pride Lands and fought Scar. Scar finally admitted that he was the one who had killed Mufasa. But Scar tried to blame the hyenas for the ruin of the Pride Lands. When the hyenas heard this, they turned on Scar. His terrible rule of the Pride Lands was over.

Later, Rafiki pointed toward Pride Rock.
"It is time," he told Simba.
Slowly, Simba walked to the place where Rafiki had held him so many years ago. He had left a frightened lion prince, but had returned a brave and wise Lion King. Simba roared to the lionesses. They roared back to their king.

Another joyous day dawned in the Pride Lands. A lion prince had been born! This time King Simba and Nala watched proudly as Rafiki held their cub high in the air.

And the Circle of Life continued.